Snapshot

by

Robert Swindells

First published in 2005 in Great Britain by
Barrington Stoke Ltd
18 Walker St, Edinburgh EH3 7LP

www.barringtonstoke.co.uk

Reprinted 2007

ISBN: 978-1-84299-347-7

Printed in Great Britain by Bell & Bain Ltd

A Note from the Author

In 2003 I had a letter from a ten-year-old boy in Walthamstow. In it there was a newspaper clipping about what had happened to him in real-life.

He'd seen a robbery and he had his camera with him, and when the robber started to drive away, he lost control of his car. The car rammed a wall very close to the young photographer. As the robber got out of the car and ran away, the lad took snapshots of him.

The boy handed his photos in to the police. As a reward, the police invited the boy to spend a day with them at Bow police station. Crimestoppers gave him a digital camera to thank him for his bravery and quick thinking.

This real-life drama was what gave me the idea for *Snapshot*.

For Vincent Parmenter, whose quick thinking gave me the idea for this book

Contents

Chapter 1

Happy Deathday

It was my birthday really, but it *could* have been my deathday. Very nearly was in fact. Name's Victor, by the way. Victor Gott. I live in Straw House. Not *a* straw house like the three little pigs – Straw House is a block of flats. We're on the third floor. Mum, Dad and me. No brothers, no sisters.

People think you're spoilt if you're an only child, but I'm not. No way. I have to do jobs for my dosh, and I don't get that much even then. I'd been saving up all year to buy one of those tiny computer cameras – a digicam. It had been like trying to push a peanut up Mount Everest with my nose. All that came to an end on my birthday. I've got this uncle, Uncle Harry, and he gave me a digicam for a present. State of the art it was too – brushed steel and the size of a matchbox. I was well chuffed. Couldn't wait to get outside and click off a few pics.

My mate Barry reckons I'm sad because I like taking pictures, but I don't care. I says to him, "better than smoking like you, or robbing, like your Tel." Barry smokes where his mum can't see him, and his big brother Tel shoplifts and picks pockets and stuff like that. He's been inside twice. What a plonker. Barry thumped me when I said that about his brother, but it's true. Taking pictures doesn't cause cancer, and they won't bang you up for it.

But taking pictures *can* be dangerous. It was for me that day ...

"Where you off to?" goes Mum. I'm by the door, putting on my hoody. I show her Uncle Harry's present – my new digicam. I wave it over my head. "Just off to take a few pics, Mum."

"What'll you take pics *of*?" she says. "There's nothing but streets out there."

"Streets are good, Mum," I tell her. "Lots of people take pictures of streets."

"Yes, and lots of people are daft," she growls. "Don't go too far, it'll be dark soon." You see – it's after school. It's teatime, and I've only just opened my cards and presents. Why do you have to go to school on your birthday? It's not right, if you ask me.

So off I went along the walkway and down the stairs. There's a lift, but it stinks and anyway it's quicker to go downstairs on foot. It was getting dark and it was drizzling. The street shone with light from shop windows and cars. The traffic was going two ways. If

I'd taken a pic, I'd have got white light from headlamps one side and red from tails and brakes the other. That's as well as amber flashes now and then. Makes a nice shot, and I think I got it just right.

Anyway there I was on the edge of the pavement, snapping away, and this car draws up and stops outside a jeweller's. Two guys get out, the one driving the car stays inside. I only started to watch them because it looked as if one of the guys was hiding something under his coat. But I was busy, didn't think too much of it. Then the shop window shattered. I looked then all right.

It was an axe the guy had inside his coat. He swung it at the jeweller's window three or four times. Glass flew. It sparkled on the pavement round his shoes. Somebody screamed. The shop door opened and two people came out. They were shouting and waving their arms in the air. The guy with the axe stepped towards them. He lifted the blade in front of their faces. They stopped dead in their tracks like scared characters in a film cartoon. The second guy was reaching into the window now. He was scooping up trays of rings and watches. I was so shocked I didn't even think about my camera. Seconds passed by before I did think about taking a photo. One of the men had his arms full of all the trays from the jewellers' smashed window. He was dumping them in the boot of his car. The other man was walking backwards, snarling at the shop assistants and waving his axe ...

I got four shots. The two guys as they scrambled back into the car. The driver as he yelled at them to get a move on. The car as it began to move off, with the axeman's head and arm still outside. The last pic was of the car coming straight at me.

And that's why I said happy deathday before. The driver had spotted me and my camera. Smile please – only he wasn't smiling.

He was bent low over the steering wheel, hunched up like some sort of pyscho.

The car came up onto the kerb towards me. I stood frozen till it was nearly too late. At the very last second, as the car's front wheels bounced up onto the kerb, I ducked behind a postbox. The side of the car crumpled as it hit the postbox. The wing-mirror flew spinning past my head. The driver clashed his gears, backed off and the car roared away. I sat on the pavement and was shaking so much I had to cling onto the box. A woman tapped me on the back. "Are you all right, dear?" she asked.

Chapter 2
Did You Get His Number?

"Y – yeah, I'm fine," I said as I sat, crouched behind the postbox. I didn't *feel* all that fine. But people were staring at me. I hate it when everyone looks at you. All I wanted was to get away from there. The woman who had tapped me on the back shook her head. "You're white as a sheet dear, I expect it's the shock. Did you get the car's number?" she asked.

"Huh? What? No, I didn't think of it." I was still shaking.

A guy steps forward. He's like, "*I* got it, scribbled it down." He waves a little notebook. "I always carry this, because you never know." You could tell he thought he was smarter than anyone there. The woman nodded. "Got a phone as well, I suppose?"

"Of course."

"Ring 999 then."

"Done it. The police are on their way."

"Why didn't I guess?" the woman said. Then she turned round and said to everyone who was watching, "You better all wait. The police'll want statements."

I wasn't going to wait. As soon as she'd turned her back, I slipped away. There's an alley that runs between two shops just there. It leads through to the next street. Somebody yelled "Oi!" as I headed for the dark, but then I was off like a rat up a drainpipe. They'd no chance of catching me. I was born here, know this bit of town like the back of my hand.

Don't get me wrong. I'm not an enemy of the police. That's not why I ran. I knew there was vital evidence inside my camera. Photos that would be very useful to the police. I knew I should hand them over.

But there was a problem. *Two* problems really. One, I was dying to see the photos myself. That meant I had to get the camera to Uncle Harry because his computer's got the right software. And two, I knew who one of the guys was – the guy who liked to do his shopping through broken windows. You won't need three guesses at his name. It was Tel Watford, my mate Barry's brother. Remember him?

Poor old Tel. Yes, I *know* he's a criminal, but he's such a sad one. Two cans short of a six pack my dad says. People take advantage. They run off, leave him to take the blame. Like I said, he's already been inside twice. I don't want to be the one to put him away again. His brother's my best *mate*, for pete's sake.

9

Anyway, that's why I ran off instead of sticking around to do my duty as an honest citizen. But it wasn't long before I wished I'd stayed.

I came out the far end of the alley, turned right and walked away, cool as you like. Nobody had chased me, I knew they wouldn't. I walked along a bit, hung another right and then another. I was back on my own street, about 200 metres down from the postbox where it had all started. It had stopped drizzling. I could see blue flashing lights outside the jeweller's.

I was well and truly over the shakes. In fact I was feeling so cool I decided I'd stroll back to the jeweller's, but on the other side of the road, to see what was going on. I'd put my hood up so no-one would see it was me. It was when I stopped for a second to do this that I sussed I was being followed.

He was wearing a dark baseball cap and a puffer jacket. He was about 20 metres behind me. Every time I stopped, he stopped. The last time he stopped was outside William Hill's betting shop. I knew it. I passed it every day. Its window is blanked out, nothing to see. Yet the guy just stood there and looked into the glass as if some drop-dead gorgeous bird was taking a bath in there. That was a dead giveaway. I moved on, glanced behind me. He was still following.

I wasn't worried. Bit excited in fact. It's not every day you fall into a real-life adventure and like I said, I know this bit of town like the back of my hand. I could shake him off anytime I chose. I'd let him shadow me for a bit, then I'd lose him.

I knew what he was after, and why he wanted it. He was after my camera, and he wanted it because he was one of the jewel thieves. Was he the driver? Or the one with the axe? I hadn't got much of a look at their faces, but the camera might have. The guy behind me didn't fancy a stretch inside, so he thought he'd trash the evidence – the pics inside my digicam. After all, how hard can it be to take a camera off a kid?

Harder than you think, I said to myself. The first plan I had was to make him follow me into one of the blocks on our estate. They're like rabbit warrens if you don't know them. Everybody gets lost. Then I thought, *No, he'll count on catching me by myself so he can scare me or wrestle the camera off me. All I have to do is stay on the streets. He won't dare tackle me in front of hundreds of people.*

So that's what I did. I walked the streets at random. I didn't use alleys of course, or cross any waste ground. I kept stopping to look in windows. That kept him on his toes. It must have driven him mad. I suppose I knew deep down I was playing a dangerous game. I didn't know then *how* dangerous. If I'd known who I was messing with I'd have given him the camera *and* asked if he'd like my left arm to go with it.

Chapter 3

Only Had it Half an Hour

I began to work out that the guy who was following me wasn't just any old hit and run criminal when I found I couldn't shake him off. That was the first clue that he wasn't just one of Tel's dodgy mates. I tried every trick in the book and he still stuck to me like glue.

Something's not right, I told myself. *This guy's smart, and that's not the sort of guy that hangs out with Tel Watford.*

It was six o'clock. The game wasn't funny anymore. I knew it'd be a bad mistake to let my shadow see where I lived, whoever he was. On the other hand, Mum'd go crazy if I stayed out any longer. Only thing left for me was to head for Straw House and hope the maze of stairs and walkways would fool him.

As I pushed open the swing doors at the bottom of the stairs to my block, I looked back quickly. The guy following me was about 50 metres behind me. He was walking fast and he had his hands in his pockets. He'd stopped pretending he wasn't interested, he was looking straight at me. I slipped inside, letting the doors bang behind me.

I thought about taking the lift, but everything it does is really, *really* slow. You punch the *door close* button and the lift thinks about it for ages. Then it obeys like it's on sleeping pills. What I did was this – I leaned in and pressed *number seven*. That's the top floor. Then I set off up the stairs.

I left the lift to slowly work out what I'd asked it to do. With a bit of luck, the guy following me would get to the lift just as the doors closed. The lights above the lift doors would show him the lift was headed for the top floor. He'd think I was in the lift. He might wait for the lift to come back down or he might go up the stairs. But he wouldn't find me. My plan was to hide on the second floor landing, in the little room where the rubbish chute is.

My plan might not work. If the guy checked out all the doors, I'd be stuffed. There was no way out of the room, except down the chute itself. I didn't know if this guy was part of the smash-and-grab team, but I was still sure he was after my camera. Or rather, the pics inside it. But I'd made up my mind now. *He was never going to get my snapshots, whatever happened.*

Halfway up the first lot of stairs, I stopped for a second and popped the smart-card out of the camera. I slipped it down the inside of my trainer. If the guy caught me, I'd hand over the empty camera. I hoped he wouldn't check it.

As I carried on up the stairs, I heard the lift come rumbling by. I can't see through concrete, so I didn't know whether my shadow was in it or not. I hoped he was. If not, he wasn't far behind me.

I didn't make it as far as the second floor. There was no bulb in the light on the first floor landing, and there in the gloom stood my old pal, Smiffy, and his two mates, Fisto and Gonoff.

"Hello, Vic old son," goes Smiffy. "We was asking what'd happened to you, weren't we lads?"

Gonoff nodded. "Ain't seen you for ages, Vic. What's that you've got anyway?"

"Just a camera." Smiffy was mostly into nicking mobiles. I hoped he wouldn't be interested in cameras.

Smiffy grinned. "*Just* a camera, Vic old lad? *Just?*" He held out a hand. "Lemme look." I knew I had no choice, so handed it over.

Smiffy whistled. "This ain't *just a camera*, my son. I seen these in Boots, 200 quid each. And you say it's just a camera. You just don't know about cutting edge technology, that's your trouble." He smirked. "Deserves an owner wot appreciates it, instrument like this. What d'you say, lads?"

The muggers nodded. "That's it," goes Fisto. "Wasted on a fella like Vic."

"Wasted," Gonoff said, like he was Fisto's echo.

"Tell you what," says Smiffy. "Me and my mates here, we'll take this fine digi off you, and as you've been so good to us, we'll let you keep your mobi, how's that?"

"Not good," I goes. I know it won't work but I try to talk them out of it. "This camera's a birthday pressie. From my uncle. I've only had it half an hour."

Smiffy smiled. "Didn't know it was your *birfday,* Vic," he said. He turned to the others. "Hear that lads, it's Vic's birfday. I fink that calls for a song, don't you?"

Both his friends nodded. They began to sing out of tune,

"Happy birfday to you

Happy birfday to you

Happy birfday, dear Victor

Happy birfday to you."

As their voices echoed away up the stairwell, Smiffy jerked his head. "Go on son, off you go. Before I ask how old you are and bang your head on the step, one bang for each year."

I wished I'd been brave enough to smash my fist into his face, one smash for each year. Instead it was taking me all my time not to cry.

I turned away and went on up the stairs. Would I bump into the guy that had been following me?

What I didn't know then was that Smiffy and I would never meet again.

Chapter 4

Just Like That

I'd got to the second floor landing when there was a loud bang. All noises echo round in these blocks. Sneeze on the first floor, some old bird on the seventh'll yell at you. But this bang really was loud. Then I heard Fisto shout, "No, no, no."

I didn't give a stuff about Fisto and his mates. I'd most likely have ignored the noise and dodged into the second floor rubbish chute room to hide before my shadow showed up. But then my brain started to put things together. My shadow. The camera. A shot.

I ran out to the walkway and looked down. A man had just left the flats and was hurrying away. Guy in a puffer jacket and a baseball cap.

I went back to the stairs and ran down. I could hear Fisto moaning. When I got to the first floor I saw Smiffy sprawled face down on the floor. The other two were staring at him. They didn't look as hard as when I last seen them. Fisto's cheeks shone with tears and Gonoff's mouth was open, like something you see down the fish market. He heard me and looked up.

"He shot him, Vic. Come up the stairs and shot him, just like that. Took the camera." He sniffled. "I fink he's dead."

I looked down at Smiffy. I'd never seen anyone dead before. There was a wet stain on his back, the size of a C.D. It was just below his left shoulder blade. I nodded.

"I think he's dead, too, Gonoff. Have you called the Bill?" I said.

Maybe I sounded really cool, but I wasn't. I wasn't. I was thinking how I'd played games with the guy who'd done this. I'd led him all over the place. For fun. And all the time he'd had a gun in his pocket. He'd have used the gun on me if he'd got me by myself. Instead of Smiffy, it could be *me* going cold on the concrete.

Gonoff was shaking his head. "No, 'course I haven't called the Bill. We don't talk to Bill, Fisto and me. In fact we'd better scarper." He looked at Fisto. "Come on mate, nothing we can do here."

"Hang on." I look hard at him. "You can't just walk away, not from this. It's murder. You saw it happen. You're eyewitnesses. The police'll have questions ..."

"I know," goes Fisto. "That's the whole point. We start answering questions and before you know it, they've got all sorts on us. They might say *we* done this – killed our own mate." He breaks off, looks at me. "What's in that camera, for pete's sake? Why did that guy *kill* for it?"

I shrugged. "Dunno. I saw a raid, at a jeweller's. Took some pics. Maybe it was that ... Anyway, it's no good you doing a runner. The cops know you're always with Smiffy. They'd pick you up, then it really *would* look as if you'd done it." I took out my mobile. "I'm calling them now, OK?"

"Suppose," mumbles Fisto. So I thumbed the three nines.

I didn't ring the cops for Smiffy, or for justice, or because it was my duty. I done it because I could feel that smart-card in my shoe. The guy with the gun'd soon find the card wasn't in the camera and he'd know who'd got it. He'd be back and I wanted a whole swarm of policemen between him and me when he was.

The copper who picked up my call thought I was winding him up at first. He's like, "Straw House, you say? And you'd be the big bad wolf, I suppose?" Took me over a minute to convince him. Moved pretty fast once I had, though.

It was the same when Mum rang. She rang two seconds after I'd talked to the copper.

"Where the heck *are* you?" she goes. "It's after seven, your tea's ruined."

"I'm downstairs, Mum, with a body." Good line, that, if you ever get a chance to use it. She's like, "*Body*? What you *talking* about, you daft little bleater? What games are you playing? Get yourself up here, quick-sticks, or I'll send your dad down to get you."

I suppose it's a rotten thing to say, what with Smiffy lying there dead and all that, but the next hour was really exciting.

Chapter 5
Moved Him Have You?

Bee-baa, bee-baa, bee-baa. I *loved* doing that noise when I was a kid. Police siren. We stood and listened as the police cars came closer. This time the sound was for real. No-one was playing at cops and robbers now.

We get lots of police sirens on the estate, I'm not saying we don't. You hear them a lot, but you don't often find out who called them, or why. We knew this time. It felt weird. To me, anyway. Fisto and Gonoff have both been in the back seats of police cars a few times. It was different for them.

Next up, we heard the clatter of boots on concrete. I relaxed a bit – my shadow wasn't going to show up now, not with the Bill about and all. We watched the stairs. Two coppers ran up to us. They were puffing and panting. They took a quick look at Smiffy. Then one came over to us.

"Which one of you's Victor Gott?"

"That's me," I said.

"You're the one who called us?"

"Yes."

The policeman looked at Fisto and Gonoff. "And what about you two? Why are *you* here?"

Gonoff nodded towards Smiffy's body. "We're his mates. We saw the bloke shoot him."

"Moved him, have you?"

"N ... no."

"Touched anything?"

"No."

"Don't. This is a crime scene. I'll get your details while we're waiting."

What are we waiting for? I asked myself. The second cop had bent down beside Smiffy. He looked at his mate and shook his head. I knew what that meant. Seen it on telly. It meant Smiffy was dead. I could've told them that, but I guess it was official now. Smiffy wasn't Smiffy anymore, he was the body.

While the first policeman was getting our names and addresses, the other one talked into his radio. He was doing that when we heard footsteps coming down and Mum turned up. The first cop went over to her and stopped her on the bottom step. "You can't come any further, madam, this is a crime scene."

Mum looked furious. She's like, "I don't *want* to come any further, I want *him* home, his tea's cold." She stabbed a finger at me.

"We'll have finished with him in a moment," says the officer. "For now, I mean."

Mum had just gone back up when two more coppers arrived. They had a reel of that blue and white tape they cordon off crime scenes with. It had POLICE DON'T CROSS printed all over it. The coppers hung the tape across where Mum had been standing. Then they stuck some across the top of the first flight of stairs. The landing was now cordoned off.

I was still waiting to get to the important bit. The smart-card was still in my shoe. I was waiting for the right moment to tell them about it. To be honest, I didn't know when the right moment would be but it didn't feel like now. Then a policeman in plain clothes showed up and I knew. I'd been waiting for a proper detective.

His name was Detective Sergeant Pitt. "Excuse me," I said, "can I have a word?"

His eyebrows went up as he muttered, "What is it, son?"

"I think I know why Smiffy ... Mr Smith was shot, sir."

He made a face at me. "Do you now? And why was he shot, son?"

"For this." I stuck two fingers down into my trainer and tweezered the smart-card out. The detective looked at it closely. He frowned. "The gunman wanted this, you think? Why was it in your shoe and not in the camera?"

"He was following *me,* sir, before he got to Smiffy. I took the card out of the camera and

hid it in my trainer in case he caught me.
I didn't know he had a gun."

Then, of course, I had to tell the detective
the whole story. I told him about the pics I'd
taken of the smash-and-grab robbery and all
the rest of it. The detective tut-tutted and
shook his head when I got to the bit about
how I tried all sorts of dodges on the gunman.
But, like I said, *I* didn't know he was a
gunman, did I?

I was lucky. He let me go home when I'd
finished my story. Fisto and Gonoff were
being taken to the police station for more
questioning. I'd had to explain how Smiffy
came to have my camera, so maybe that's
why the police held onto Fisto and Gonoff.

I was in big trouble when I got in. They'd
had macaroni cheese for tea. Mine was like
the bottom of a plastic flip-flop now. Mum
showed it to me, then chucked it in the bin.
I had to make myself some beans on toast.

Much nicer than macaroni cheese any day if you ask me, but I wasn't daft enough to say so.

Dad's like, "Your Uncle Harry should've had more sense than to give a kid your age a camera. Kid your age hasn't a clue what to photograph. Fancy, taking snaps of a robbery. Didn't you stop to think it might be a silly thing to do? D'you think robbers would let some kid put them away for years on end?" He snorted. "What if they find out where you live, eh? What if they come here, with their guns and their axes? What if they have a go at your mum? You won't feel so clever then, I'll bet."

I hadn't thought of that. Detective Pitt had kept the smart-card, but the gunman didn't know that. What if he *did* come? He'd killed poor Smiffy just like that, as if shooting a lad was the same as stamping on a beetle. And it wasn't even Smiffy who'd made a prat out of him, it was me.

We watched telly all evening, but I didn't enjoy it. Couldn't relax. I was listening to every little noise, and ours is a very noisy block.

It was even worse in bed. I kept my bedside light on and I put my phone under my pillow. Still, it was well after midnight when I dropped off.

Chapter 6

Two in One Day

"Vic. *Victor*." I woke up. Dad was shaking me. It was still dark outside.

"Whassup?" I mumbled. "What time is it, Dad?"

"It's early, son. Listen. I want you to tell this man what you did with the card from that camera."

"*Man*?" I woke up then all right. There was a man behind Dad. He looked enormous in my small bedroom and was wearing a puffer jacket and a dark baseball cap.

Mum was there too. She looked very scared.

I sat up without taking my eyes off the guy. He gave Dad a push to move. Then he stood over me. "Where is the card?"

"Don't hurt him, please," goes Mum. "He's only a child."

"Shut up." He was staring in my eyes. "Where is it, little boy?"

"Uh ... I gave it to the Bill." Man, was I scared. I wished I had the card so I could let him have it. Then he'd get out of our flat. Dad had been right. I'd been really stupid and I didn't feel clever at all now.

"Bill?" goes the guy. "Who is Bill?"

"The police."

"Ah!" He nods, slides a gun out of his pocket.

"I *told* you," said Dad. "He's a kid, he was scared, they took it off him."

"Shut your stupid mouth," the man snapped.

He turned to Dad and Mum. "Face down on the floor, now."

"What you gonna do?" Dad's voice was a croak. "You can't ...

"Can't I?" The man turned back to me. "You also, face down, quick," he said.

It wasn't real, I felt like I was in a nightmare. Everything went into slow motion except my brain. Getting out of bed I saw the clock on my bedside unit. It was ten past three. I thought, *twelve hours from now I'll just be coming out of school*. But I knew I wouldn't. There'd be no more school for me. My mate Barry would read about it in the paper, what happened to the Gotts. It'd be like something on the telly. Neighbours would be shaking their heads, saying we were quiet people, kept ourselves to ourselves.

"Let the boy go," says Dad into the carpet. "And my wife. What good will it do to ...?"

"I told you, shut up," the man hissed back at him.

I got down on all fours beside Mum. Then, as I lay down, she lifted her arm and put it over my back. I turned my head sideways so I could look at her. So she'd be the last thing I seen. She was crying, without making a sound. The carpet smelled dusty. There was a sharp click. That must be the guy doing something with the gun. I thought, *it'll be now*.

Everything exploded in light and noise. I thought that was it. That was what it was like being shot. But it wasn't. It wasn't, because the noise and the light didn't stop. Didn't go black or silent. Now there were voices, shouting. Heavy footsteps thumped on the carpet, made my head judder. There were shots – four I think. Then somebody cried out and something fell over with a crash. Mum's arm lifted off me and as I opened my eyes, I saw the room was full of men.

Somebody lifted me up. I was on the bed and I was looking at something on the floor. I never seen a dead body in my life, now I seen two in one day. The gunman, my shadow, lay with his jacket half off and my bedside unit across his legs. He looked surprised, which I suppose he was. I was a bit surprised myself.

Everything was confusion at first. People coming and going. Snatches of talk I didn't understand. I remember having a three-way hug with Mum and Dad, which was a first. And a mug of cocoa, which wasn't. Uncle Harry was there for some reason, even though it was the middle of the night. Maybe Dad got him over to give him hell about the digicam. If so it didn't work, because he told me not to worry, he'd get me another camera.

After a long, long time, everybody went away, and Mum, Dad and I were on our own at last. It was after four in the morning and I was shattered. All I wanted was sleep. My room was cordoned off though, like the first floor landing. Crime scene. The guys in white'd be back in the morning to poke through everything.

I slept in my parents' bed. It was like being two years old again. Dad stayed up. He said he might as well get a good start on the day. Said he couldn't sleep anyway.

I didn't have any trouble.

Chapter 7
Coco Pops in Bed

Next day was Friday. It was a school day, but I thought I could swing myself a day off. Well, I'd not had my ration of sleep, had I? Plus I'd been through a hard time. When Mum came to get me up I was ready with my plan. She called from the doorway. I didn't stir. She came in, called louder. I lay still. She bent down to give me a nudge. The second her hand touched me I jumped up suddenly and shouted out like this, "Yeeeaaaaagh!"

"Sorry," she gasps. "Sorry Vic, it's only me. Time to get up."

I shook my head, let out a long, dramatic sigh. "Wow, Mum, you nearly scared me to death. I thought it was that guy ..."

"I know love, and I'm really sorry. I don't want you to be late for school, that's all."

"S ... school?" I frowned up at her. "I ... don't think I can handle school today, Mum. I'm wrecked, nerves all shot. I need total rest. And some Coco Pops in bed."

I shouldn't have added the bit about Coco Pops. I was doing fine till then. Mum laughed and peeled back my duvet. "Come on, young man, shake a leg. There's going to be people all over the flat today. It'll be bad enough, without *you* getting in the way."

I didn't need to be told that. I *knew* there'd be people. That's why I wanted to be there. But it was no good. At ten past eight I was getting into the train as I always did, with my Coco Pops inside me and my lunch in my bag.

Barry always gets on at the stop after me. I put my bag on the seat as always, to save it for him. I wouldn't be there to watch the detectives but, hey, I had a seriously good story to tell my mate.

"Hello Vic," Barry muttered when he got on the train.

"Hi Barry." I looked at him. "Something the matter?"

"You could say that."

"Why, what's happened?" I asked.

He shook his head. "It's our Tel."

"Oh." I knew what he was going to say. It sounds bad, but I'd forgotten all about poor Tel after everything that happened with Smiffy. I was just glad I hadn't told the Bill I'd clocked him on the smash-and-grab. "In bother again, is he?"

"Yeah." Barry stared out of the window. "Only went and smashed a jeweller's window, didn't he? In a stolen motor. With two other guys."

"And they was nicked?"

Barry snorted. "*He* was. Our Tel. The other two scarpered, left him to drive the car onto waste ground and torch it."

"And did he?"

"Oh yeah. He drove it onto waste ground all right. Just one snag. The place he found was dead opposite a bleatin' police station. Second the car goes up in flames, the coppers come running out and grab him. And now Tel's like, 'You don't grass your mates up, it's rule number one.' That means he'll go down and his mates can flog all the Rolex watches without him."

I shook my head. "Not this time, mate."

"Huh? How d'you mean?"

So I told him my story, starting with the smash-and-grab.

"So you see," I smiled when I'd finished, "those two guys're on Vic's candid camera with your bro. They'll go down *without* Tel having to grass them up."

Barry nodded. "Well, at least that's something." He frowned. "But who the heck was the guy with the gun? Was he one of Tel's mates too?"

I shrugged. "Dunno. I took some other pics, y'know, up and down the street? Before I saw the robbery. Maybe I got something without knowing it. Something important."

Barry looked at me. "Have to be something really important, wouldn't it? To make someone want to kill and kill again?"

I had no answer to that. The train clacked and swayed us to school, and I didn't tell anybody about what had happened. I don't like people looking at me. Maybe if I said nothing, only Barry would ever know.

Fat chance.

Chapter 8

Like Grass Growing

That day was Friday. It dragged even more than Fridays always do. I couldn't stop thinking about what was going on at Straw House. What were they doing in my bedroom? What would they be looking for? They didn't need clues about the gunman. He was on a slab down the mortuary and going nowhere. What were they looking for then?

And what about my snapshots? What had happened to them? I'd given my smart-card to Detective Sergeant Pitt after Smiffy was shot. They'd have examined them by now.

Did they show anything? Was there something my shadow wanted so badly he lost his life trying to get it back? What could it be?

The day didn't half drag on. But, at last, half-three snailed by and school packed up for the weekend. Me and Barry got the ten to four train and sat talking about all those questions till we got to Barry's stop. After that I stared out of the window. *Can you ever get to sleep in a room where a guy's been shot to death?* I asked myself.

When I got home I had to use the lift because the first floor landing was still cordoned off.

"Aw, come *on*," I groaned as the lift started to go up slowly, like grass growing. *I'd be quicker if I climbed the lift-shaft*, I thought. I hoped my room wasn't still a crime scene, or I'd be kipping in with my parents again.

"It's all right son," goes Mum before I get a chance to ask. "They've gone."

"What happened, Mum, did they find anything?"

She shook her head. "Well, *I* don't know, do I? They didn't tell me anything. I was only here to let them in and make cups of tea."

"Did they say anything about my snapshots?"

"I *told* you, Vic, they didn't say anything. Oh, except we can get you a new carpet and claim the money."

"New carpet?"

"Yes, they've taken the old one away because *he* died on it."

"Glad he didn't die on the *bed,* then. I like my bed!"

Nothing much happened for weeks after that. The police finished on the first floor landing and took the tape away. It was in the local paper how Smiffy got shot in Straw House, and how they couldn't have his funeral because the police were still working on the case. There wasn't anything about me or my shadow. Some nosey kids stopped me in the yard and asked me what I'd seen because I lived near the murder scene. I said I didn't know any more than they did, and they left me alone.

Then, just when I thought it had all died down, two important looking police officers came to our flat.

It was a Friday, seven at night. Dad was out. Mum and me were watching telly. Suddenly there was this really loud knock at the door. Mum cracked it open on the chain and there they were. Civvy kit, I.D. cards. Detective Chief Inspectors Lawson and Gill. She let them in, made me turn the TV off. They looked at me and Lawson's like, "Is your name Victor, young man?"

"Yes, sir," I says.

"Well, Victor," he said. "My friend and I have come to thank you."

"*Me?*" I goes, and he smiled and said, "Yes, Victor, you."

So Mum sat them down, put the kettle on and this is what Lawson told us.

"We got your snapshots up on screen straight after you'd given Sergeant Pitt the smart-card. We looked hard at them. There were some good shots of the smash-and-grab robbery, but we didn't think the shooting was anything to do with that. We thought you must have caught something more serious by mistake. At first we couldn't see anything else important in your photos. They were just photos of a wet street, people walking in the rain and passing traffic. We ran them again, and this time we spotted something. Or rather, someone."

Lawson broke off, smiled and sipped his tea. Gill took over.

"You'd snapped the entrance to an underground station just as a man was coming out. We thought we'd seen the fellow before, in a photo that the security services had sent out to all police stations. When we had the snap enlarged, all hell broke loose. The man was Vladek Topp. You won't have heard of him, but he's wanted by the police forces of at least 15 countries. He's a terrorist who's known for his attacks on subway systems. He fills them with poisonous gas." Gill pulled a face. "And you caught him coming out of the underground."

"Oh, no," goes Mum. "Had he ...?"

"No no." Gill shook his head. "He hadn't planted anything. He was probably having a good look round to see where the best place would be. You know, for maximum damage, to hurt the most people ..." Mum shivered and Gill went on.

49

"We got in touch with the security services straight away. The same evening, they carried out raids on a few houses they'd been watching. In one house they found 50 gas canisters hidden in the cellar. Cyanide gas. That's a killer when it's pumped underground."

Then Lawson started talking again. "The people across the street from the house said they'd seen a man leaving the house that day. He was tall and wore a puffer jacket and a dark baseball cap. Like the man in your photo."

Mum looked at the two officers. "This Vladek character – is he the one that ...?" she began to ask.

Gill nodded. "Yes, he's the fellow who shot Jimmy Smith on your stairs. Later he broke into your home. He'd seen Victor take his photograph, disastrous for a wanted killer. He knew the security services knew his face already. He'd have stopped at nothing to get your photo back."

"Yes, but ..." I said. "How come you guys knew Topp was in our flat?"

Gill shook his head. "We didn't. We asked ourselves why he'd left the safe house. He couldn't have known we were about to raid it. We thought he must have gone after the smart-card."

"But he didn't know where I lived."

"We think he must have, son."

"How?"

"Well, Topp must have found the camera was empty a minute or two after you saw him leaving the block after shooting Smith. He *had* to get that smart-card. So he came back. When the police arrived to look at Smith, Topp must have hidden somewhere in Straw House. We don't know where he was while you were talking to the police, but he must

have been somewhere he could watch where
you went afterwards. He couldn't do anything
with the police everywhere, so he waited and
hid. Then he came to your flat later."

"Ah."

"Anyway, Victor," said Lawson, who had
finished his tea, "the point is that you saved
the lives of hundreds of people on the
underground. You and that camera of yours.
That reminds me ..." He fished in his pocket
and pulled out my digicam. "Is this it?"

"Hey, yeah, looks like it. Where'd you ...?"

Lawson grinned. "Your shadow dropped it
in a shop doorway and some honest citizen
handed it in. Here." He passed it to me, as
well as a long buff envelope. I looked at the
envelope. "What's this?"

"It's ... er ... a little something to say
thank you from .... well, from some people

who think you did very well. Open it when we've gone."

They left nearly straight away, and Mum gave me a hug. "Our hero," she says. "Aren't you going to open it?"

I did. Inside was a cheque for 500 pounds and a note that said, *Sorry about all the fuss with the press.* Mum frowned. "*What* fuss with the press? We haven't *had* any fuss."

Talk about speaking too soon.

Chapter 9
Three Cheers

When Dad came in he had to have the whole story, then a drink to celebrate. It was late when I got to bed in the room of death. I've never *seen* the ghost of Vladek Topp, but it's there all right.

Half-six next morning they arrived. Reporters, photographers. On the walkway outside the flat. Dad had to shove guys aside when he left for work. Mum bolted the door when he'd gone, and even then someone shoved a hand-mic through the letterbox.

"Victor, a few words for your public, please," he yells. I went and hid under the bed. On my new carpet. Nightmare.

Mum phoned school, would they excuse me today. The Head said it was ridiculous, holding a child prisoner in his flat. He said he'd phone the papers to protest.

If he phoned them, it did no good. The walkway stayed jam-packed. Reporters took turns knocking on the door, and we had to leave the phone off the hook.

By lunchtime Mum had had enough. She called Uncle Harry. He's good in a crisis, always seems to know what's best to do. He came round, pushed his way through them all and picked a reporter at random. "Want an exclusive?" he asked her. She did, and he hustled her inside. Only then did the reporters and cameras start to move away.

She was called Pippa. She worked on the *Star* and was nice. She knelt on my new carpet and asked me some questions. I stayed under the bed. After a bit I came out. By the time she left, the walkway was empty.

You should've seen next day's *Star.* Mum lent Pippa my school photo and there it was, all over the front page. They'd enlarged it about 600 times, and I had a face as big as the town hall clock. SNAPSHOT SUPERBOY SCOOPS SPOOKS yelled the headline, in enormous letters.

Then I had to go to school. "Hey!" goes some plonker, as soon as me and Barry walk in the yard. "It's Snapshot Superboy and his faithful friend."

And if you think *that's* bad, the Head decided it would be really cool to get me up on the platform in assembly and have three cheers. I'm not kidding – three flipping cheers. I nearly died.

It's a bit better now, thank goodness. The smash-and-grab lads are all doing time. They don't know I snapped 'em, and I'm glad. I didn't want to turn my mate's brother in. There's worse guys in the world than Tel Watford.

But I hope none of them walks into *my* shot again, that's all.

Barrington Stoke would like to thank all its readers for commenting on the manuscript before publication and in particular:

Aroomza Aslam

Charlotte Barnett

William Blanchard

Josie Bond

Rachael Boon

Katy Burke

Ann Campbell

Oli Carroll

Alistair Chalmers

Linda Dolan

Sarah Dunn

Rory Hurren

Anthony Lawrence

Greig Linton

Ashley McCallum

Emma McIntosh

Mrs Alwin Martin

Chris Mengham

Shannen Neeves

Ruth Patton

Daniel Pearce

Iain Petrie

Denise Williams

Jayce Wilson

Jane Wintle

Become a Consultant!

Would you like to give us feedback on our titles before they are published? Contact us at the email address below – we'd love to hear from you!

info@barringtonstoke.co.uk
www.barringtonstoke.co.uk